OUR GOVERNMENT

The Supreme Court

by Mari Schuh

BELLWETHER MEDIA · MINNEAPOLIS, MN

Blastoff! Readers are carefully developed by literacy experts to build reading stamina and move students toward fluency by combining standards-based content with developmentally appropriate text.

Level 1 provides the most support through repetition of high-frequency words, light text, predictable sentence patterns, and strong visual support.

Level 2 offers early readers a bit more challenge through varied sentences, increased text load, and text-supportive special features.

Level 3 advances early-fluent readers toward fluency through increased text load, less reliance on photos, advancing concepts, longer sentences, and more complex special features.

★ **Blastoff! Universe**

Reading Level

Grade **K**

Grades **1–3**

Grade **4**

This edition first published in 2021 by Bellwether Media, Inc.

No part of this publication may be reproduced in whole or in part without written permission of the publisher. For information regarding permission, write to Bellwether Media, Inc., Attention: Permissions Department, 6012 Blue Circle Drive, Minnetonka, MN 55343.

Library of Congress Cataloging-in-Publication Data

Names: Schuh, Mari C., 1975- author.
Title: The Supreme Court / Mari Schuh.
Description: Minneapolis, MN : Bellwether Media, Inc. 2021. | Series: Blastoff! readers. Our government | Includes bibliographical references and index. | Audience: Ages 5-8 | Audience: Grades K-1 | Summary: "Developed by literacy experts for students in kindergarten through grade three, this book introduces the Supreme Court to young readers through leveled text and related photos"–Provided by publisher.
Identifiers: LCCN 2019059277 (print) | LCCN 2019059278 (ebook) | ISBN 9781644872055 (library binding) | ISBN 9781681038292 (paperback) | ISBN 9781618919632 (ebook)
Subjects: LCSH: United States. Supreme Court–Juvenile literature. | Courts of last resort–United States–Juvenile literature.
Classification: LCC KF8742 .S287 2021 (print) | LCC KF8742 (ebook) | DDC 347.73/26–dc23
LC record available at https://lccn.loc.gov/2019059277
LC ebook record available at https://lccn.loc.gov/2019059278

Editor: Rebecca Sabelko   Designer: Laura Sowers

Printed in the United States of America, North Mankato, MN.

Table of Contents

What Is the Supreme Court?

The Supreme Court is powerful. It is the highest court in the United States!

Justice
Stephen Breyer

Justice
Elena Kagan

Justice
Neil Gorsuch

The court is part of the **judicial branch**.

Working Together

Legislative Branch	Executive Branch	Judicial Branch
writes laws	signs laws	studies laws

president

vice president

Senate   House of Representatives

Supreme Court

It has nine **justices**.
One is chief justice.
He or she leads
the group.

Chief Justice
John Roberts

The president
picks new justices.
The **Senate**
votes on them.

Justice
Neil Gorsuch

President
Donald Trump

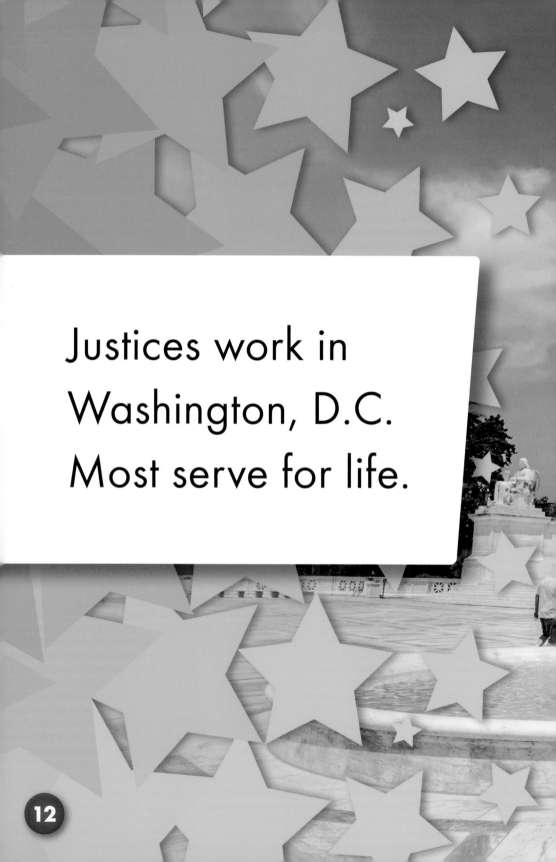

Justices work in Washington, D.C. Most serve for life.

U.S. Supreme Court building, Washington, D.C.

Duties

The court makes sure **laws** follow the **Constitution**.

**Justice
Sandra Day O'Connor**

The court hears **cases**.
It also explains laws.

drawing of 1910
U.S. Supreme Court

An Important Job

There are many
lower courts.
They all follow
the Supreme Court.

Texas Supreme
Court justices

The court makes sure laws are fair!

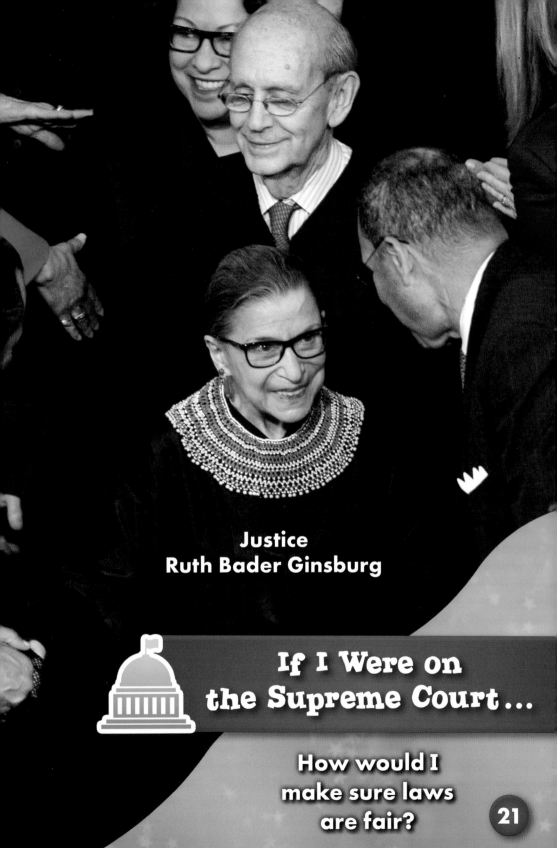

Justice
Ruth Bader Ginsburg

If I Were on the Supreme Court...

How would I make sure laws are fair?

Glossary

cases

disagreements between two groups that are decided in a court

justices

judges who serve on the Supreme Court

Constitution

a document that explains how the government works

laws

rules that people must follow

judicial branch

the part of the government that makes sure laws follow the Constitution

Senate

part of the legislative branch; the Senate makes laws.

To Learn More

AT THE LIBRARY

Murray, Julie. *Supreme Court.* Minneapolis, Minn.: Abdo Kids, 2018.

Schuh, Mari. *The United States Constitution.* Minneapolis, Minn.: Bellwether Media, 2019.

Stoltman, Joan. *20 Fun Facts about the Supreme Court.* New York, N.Y.: Gareth Stevens Publishing, 2018.

ON THE WEB

FACTSURFER

Factsurfer.com gives you a safe, fun way to find more information.

1. Go to www.factsurfer.com.

2. Enter "Supreme Court" into the search box and click 🔍.

3. Select your book cover to see a list of related content.

Index